URBAN LEGENDS
EXPOSED!

by Megan Cooley Peterson

CAPSTONE PRESS
a capstone imprint

Published by Spark, an imprint of Capstone
1710 Roe Crest Drive, North Mankato, Minnesota 56003
capstonepub.com

Copyright © 2023 by Capstone. All rights reserved. No part of this publication may be reproduced in whole or in part, or stored in a retrieval system, or transmitted in any form or by any means, electronic, mechanical, photocopying, recording, or otherwise, without written permission of the publisher.

Library of Congress Cataloging-in-Publication Data is available on the Library of Congress website

ISBN: 9781666357202 (hardcover)
ISBN: 9781666357219 (ebook PDF)

Summary: Readers will be captivated by mysterious urban legends while also learning the facts about each claim.

Editorial Credits
Editor: Mandy Robbins; Designer: Heidi Thompson; Media Researchers: Jo Miller and Pam Mitsakos; Production Specialist: Tori Abraham

Image Credits
Alamy: AGF Srl, 27; Getty Images: quavondo, 7, Tanuj Choudhary, 22; Shutterstock: AIB Photography, 10, AlbertoGonzalez, 13, ANDRANIK HAKOBYAN, 9, andreiuc88, 21, Bill Perry, 28, ChaiKetsiam, 8, Edmund Lowe Photography, 11, Gianfranco Vivi, 25, koya979, 12, Marzolino, 29, Nata Bene, 16, New Africa, 17, Raggedstone, Cover, 2, 15, stephen mulcahey, 23, STILLFX, 26, Tacio Philip Sansonovski, 19, Tobias Hauke, 18, Vladimir Mulder, 5

All internet sites appearing in back matter were available and accurate when this book was sent to press.

TABLE OF CONTENTS

Have You Heard?......................4

The Vanishing Hitchhiker.............6

The Hook 12

The Spider Bite.....................16

Ghost in the Trees..................20

Secret Tunnels......................24

    Glossary.................... 30

    Read More................... 31

    Internet Sites.............. 31

    Index....................... 32

    About the Author........... 32

Words in **bold** are in the glossary.

HAVE YOU HEARD?

Have you heard the story about alligators in the **sewer**? Or the ghost who asks for a ride? **Urban legends** are often gross or scary stories. These made-up tales are told as though they really happened. They usually warn people what not to do. But sometimes they turn out to be true!

THE VANISHING HITCHHIKER

A driver. A dark road. A **hitchhiker**. The Vanishing Hitchhiker is a famous **legend**. In the story, a man is driving home one night. He sees a young woman standing on the side of the road. He pulls over to give her a ride home.

The woman sits in the back seat. She gives her address to the driver. But when he gets there, the back seat is empty!

The driver knocks on her door. The people tell him the woman died many years ago. Had the driver given a ride to a ghost?

People around the world tell this story. The details often change. The young woman sometimes leaves a book or a scarf behind. Sometimes the driver gives the woman his jacket. He later finds it on a gravestone. In other **versions,** the driver picks up an alien.

FACT

The Vanishing Hitchhiker has been told since the 1800s. In earlier tales, a man in a horse-drawn carriage picks up the hitchhiker.

THE HOOK

One night, a couple goes for a drive. They park in the woods. A news report comes on the radio. A criminal has escaped from a local jail. He has a hook for a hand.

Suddenly, a branch scrapes the car. *Scritch-scratch*. The couple speeds away. At home, they find a hook stuck in the car door.

The Hook was first told in the United States in the 1950s. The story warned of the danger of going out at night. Some real-life couples have died while parked at night. The Hook could be based on true stories.

> **FACT**
> Urban legends are usually shared by word of mouth or social media.

THE SPIDER BITE

Not every urban legend is scary. In one gross tale, a girl goes on vacation with her family. During the trip, a bug bites her cheek. The bite won't heal. It gets bigger and redder. One day, hundreds of baby spiders crawl out of the bump.

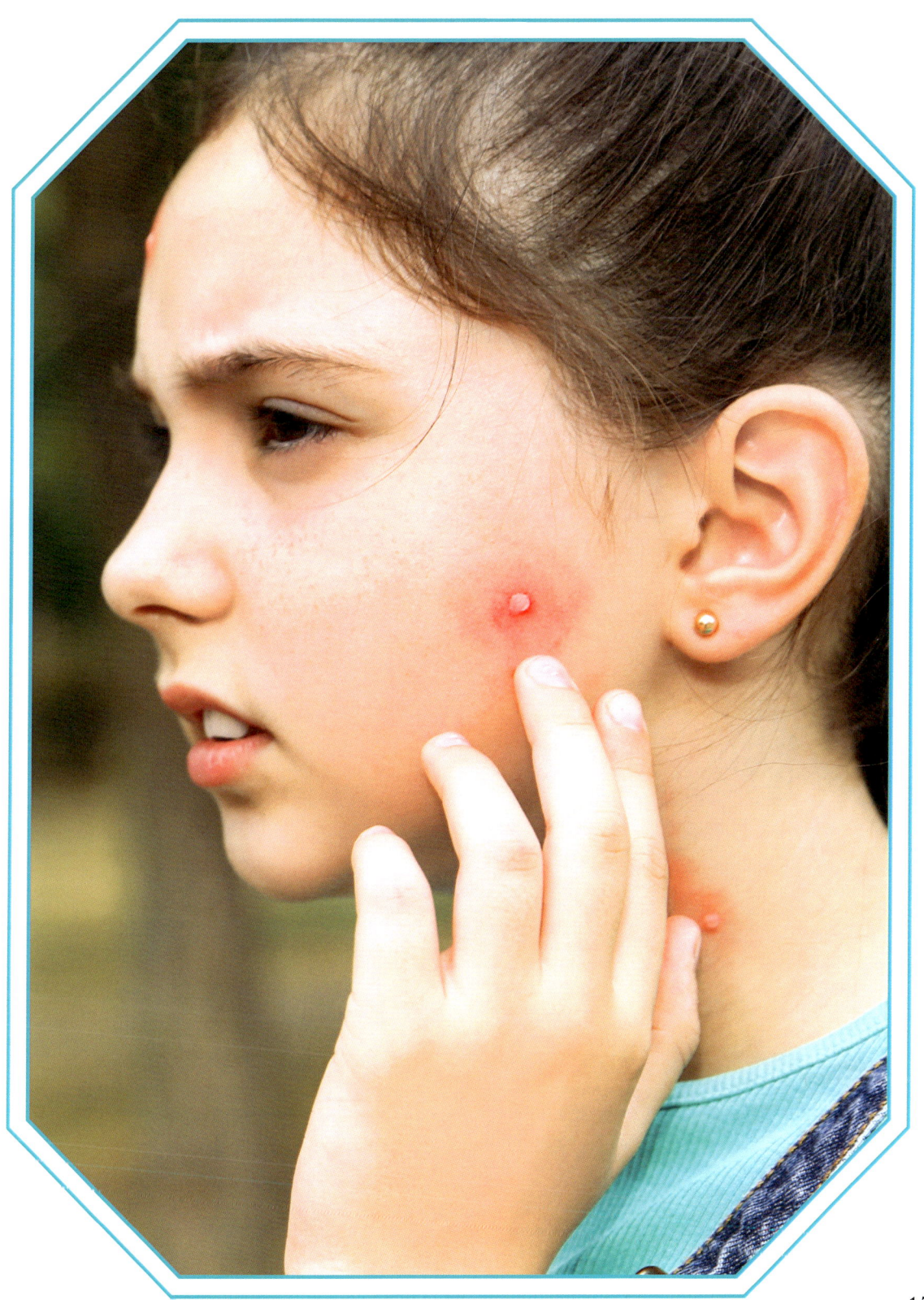

Is this spidery tale based on a true story? It might be. Spiders can't lay eggs in human skin. But some bugs can. Human botfly eggs can hatch inside a person's skin. Worm-like **larvae** wriggle out 30 days later.

a spider egg

botfly larvae

GHOST IN THE TREES

Everyone in Maules, Switzerland, knew the legend. A strange creature was said to roam the nearby woods. It was tall and wore a long cape. A gas mask kept its face hidden. Was it a person? A ghost? Or just a scary story?

In 2013, the people of Maules got their answer. Someone snapped a photo of the figure. The newspaper printed it.

Soon, a cape and gas mask were found in the woods. The person who had worn them also left a note. They were tired of being called a ghost. No one ever saw them again.

SECRET TUNNELS

For hundreds of years, people in Puebla, Mexico, passed along a legend. According to the story, tunnels ran under the city. People hid inside them during wars. No one had ever seen the tunnels. But it was still a fun tale to tell.

Puebla, Mexico

In 2014, city workers found what they thought was a sewer. But as they dug, they made an amazing discovery. The tunnels of Puebla were real! So far, they have uncovered 6 miles of stone tunnels. The tunnels are up to 22 feet high.

FACT
Toys, marbles, and kitchen items were found in the tunnels.

The tunnels of Puebla, Mexico

Workers built the first tunnel around 1531. Soldiers used them to travel between military **forts**.

Fort Loreto in Puebla, Mexico

The tunnels also connected churches. Over time, floods filled them with mud. The tunnels became a legend. What other urban legends might turn out to be true?

1863 attack on Puebla, Mexico

Glossary

fort (FORT)—a building that is well defended against attacks

hitchhiker (HICH-hiker)—a person who asks a stranger for a ride, usually in a car or other vehicle

larva (LAR-vuh)—an insect at the stage of development between an egg and an adult

legend (LEJ-uhnd)—a story handed down from earlier times that may not be completely true

sewer (SOO-ur)—a system, often an underground pipe, that carries away liquid and solid waste

urban legend (UR-buhn LEJ-uhnd)—a story about an unusual event or occurrence that many people believe is true but that is usually not true

version (VUR-zhuhn)—a different or changed form of something

Read More

Bassington, Cyril. *Legends*. New York: Gareth Stevens Publishing, 2020.

Hoena, Blake. *Creepy Urban Legends*. North Mankato, MN: Capstone Press, 2018.

Kenney, Karen Latchana. *Spine-Tingling Urban Legends*. Minneapolis: Lerner Publications, 2018.

Internet Sites

Are There Really Alligators In the Sewers?
evergladesholidaypark.com/alligators-in-the-sewer/

Can Spiders Lay Eggs In Your Skin?
woodypet.com/can-spiders-lay-eggs-in-your-skin/

The Vanishing Hitchhiker
academickids.com/encyclopedia/index.php/The_Vanishing_Hitchhiker

Index

alligators in the sewer, 4

botflies, 18, 19

ghosts, 4, 9, 20, 23

Hook, The, 12–13, 14

Maules, Switzerland, 20, 22–23

Puebla, Mexico, 24, 25, 26, 27, 28–29

spiders, 16, 18

tunnels 24, 26, 27, 28–29

Vanishing Hitchhiker, The, 4, 6, 8–10, 11

About the Author

Megan Cooley Peterson has been an avid reader and writer since she was a little girl. She has written nonfiction children's books about topics ranging from urban legends to gross animal facts. She lives in Minnesota with her husband and daughter, and cuddly kitty.